D0226983

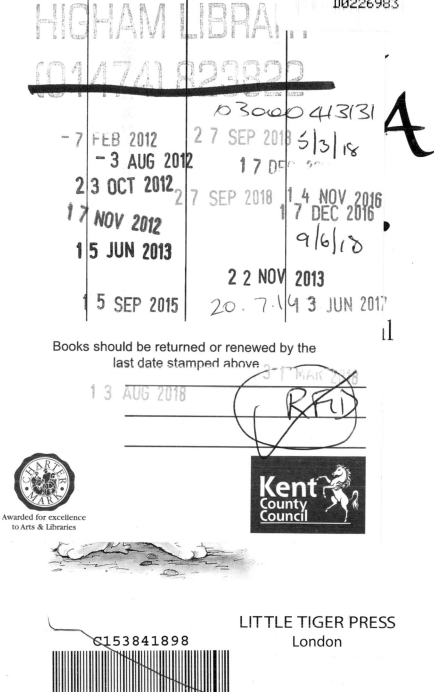

Awarded for excellence
to Arts & Libraries

Kent
County
Council

LITTLE TIGER PRESS
London

LITTLE TIGER PRESS
An imprint of Magi Publications
1 The Coda Centre, 189 Munster Road,
London SW6 6AW
www.littletigerpress.com
This volume copyright © Magi Publications 2007
All rights reserved
ISBN 978-1-84506-613-0
Printed in China
10 9 8 7 6 5 4 3 2 1

LITTLE BEAR'S SPECIAL WISH
Gillian Lobel
Illustrated by Gaby Hansen
First published in Great Britain 2003
by Little Tiger Press,
an imprint of Magi Publications
Text copyright © Gillian Lobel 2003
Illustrations copyright © Gaby Hansen 2003

THE WISH CAT
Ragnhild Scamell
Illustrated by Gaby Hansen
First published in Great Britain 2001
by Little Tiger Press,
an imprint of Magi Publications
Text copyright © Ragnhild Scamell 2001
Illustrations copyright © Gaby Hansen 2001

LITTLE BEAR'S
SPECIAL
WISH

GILLIAN LOBEL

illustrated by
GABY HANSEN

The sun was still in bed
when Little Brown Bear crept out
into the shadowy woods.

"I wish, I wish . . ." he whispered.

"You're up early, Little Brown Bear!"
called Lippity Rabbit. "What are you
wishing for?"

"It's my mummy's birthday," said
Little Brown Bear, "and I wish I could
find the most special present in all
the world for her."

"I'll help you!" said Lippity Rabbit.
So off they went along the winding
path. Little pools of moonlight danced
around their feet.

In the middle of the woods was a big rock.
Little Brown Bear sat down for a moment
to think. High above him glittered a star,
so big and bright he could almost touch it.

"I know – I could give my mummy
a star," he said. "That would be a very
special present."

Little Brown Bear
gave a little jump.
But he could not
reach the star.

He gave a very
big jump. But still
he could not
reach the star.
Then Little Brown
Bear had an idea.

"I know!" he said. "If we climb to the very top of the hill, then we will be able to reach the stars!"

From the top of the hill the stars looked even brighter – and much nearer, too. Little Brown Bear stretched up on to his tiptoes. But the stars were still too far away. Then Little Brown Bear had a very good idea indeed.

"I know!" he said. "We must build
a big, big tower to the stars!"
   "I'll help you!" said
Lippity Rabbit.

Together they piled the biggest stones
they could find, one on top of the other.
Then they stepped back and looked.
A stone stairway stretched to the stars.
   "Now I shall reach a star for my mummy,"
said Little Brown Bear happily. He climbed
right to the top and stretched out a paw.
But still he couldn't reach the stars.

"I know!" called Lippity Rabbit. "If I climb on your shoulders, then I can knock a star down with my long, loppy ears!"

Lippity Rabbit scrambled on to Little Brown Bear's shoulders. He stretched up his long, loppy ears. He waggled them furiously.

"Be careful, Lippity!" called Little Brown Bear. "You're making me wobble!"

Suddenly Little Brown Bear
felt something tapping his foot.
"Can I help you?" croaked
a voice.
"Why yes, Very Small Frog,"
said Little Brown Bear. "Are
you any good at jumping?"
Very Small Frog puffed out
his chest.
"Just watch me!" he said.
High into the air he flew, and landed right
between Lippity Rabbit's long, loppy ears.
"Can you reach the brightest star from
there?" asked Little Brown Bear.
"No problem!" shouted Very Small
Frog. "Look out, stars! Here I come!"

Very Small Frog gave a great push with his strong back legs. Up, up, up he sailed. Lippity Rabbit's long, loppy ears twirled round and round.

"Help!" he shouted. "Somebody save me!"

Backwards and forwards he swayed, and backwards and forwards swayed Little Brown Bear. With a mighty crash the stone tower toppled to the ground. And down and down tumbled Lippity Rabbit and Little Brown Bear.

"I can't breathe, Lippity!" gasped Little Brown Bear. "You're sitting right on by dose!"

Then Very Small Frog sailed down from the stars and landed on Lippity Rabbit's head.

"I'm sorry, Little Brown Bear," he said. "I jumped right over the moon, but I still couldn't reach the stars."

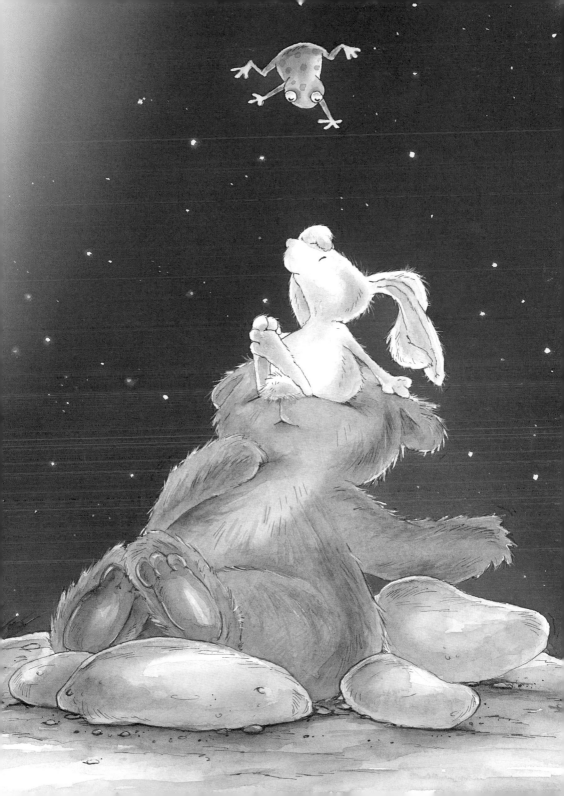

Little Brown Bear sat up carefully. His nose was scratched and his head hurt.

"Now my special wish will *never* come true," he said. "I shall never find a star for my mummy!"

"Don't be sad, Little Brown Bear," said Lippity Rabbit. And he gave him a big hug.

A tear ran down Little Brown Bear's nose, and splashed into a tiny pool at his feet.

As he rubbed his eyes, Little Brown Bear saw something that danced and sparkled in the shining water. Surely it was his star! Little Brown Bear jumped up with excitement.

"Now I know what to do!" he cried.

Off he ran
down the hillside.
"Wait for us!"
cried Lippity Rabbit
and Very Small Frog.

Through the ferny woods they ran, over the silver meadows, until they reached the stream. For a long time they hunted along the sandy shore until Little Brown Bear found just what he was looking for. Then carefully, carefully, he carried it all the way home.

"Happy birthday, Mummy!" he cried.

Into his mother's lap he placed a pearly shell. There, in the heart of the shell, a tiny pool of water quivered. And in that pool a very special star shimmered and shook.

"Lippity Rabbit and Very Small Frog helped me find the shell, but I caught the star all by myself!" said Little Brown Bear proudly.

Mother Bear knelt down and gave him a big hug. "Thank you all very much," she said. "This is a very special birthday present indeed!"

The
Wish
Cat

Ragnhild Scamell

illustrated by Gaby Hansen

Holly's house had a cat flap.
It was a small door in the big
door so a cat could come and go.
But Holly didn't have a cat.

One night, something magical
happened. Holly saw a falling star.
As the star trailed across the sky,
she made a wish.

"I wish I had a kitten," she
whispered. "A tiny cuddly kitten
who could jump in and out of
the cat flap."

CRASH!

Something big landed on the window sill outside. It wasn't a kitten . . . It was Tom, the scruffiest, most raggedy cat Holly had ever seen. He sat there in the moonlight, smiling a crooked smile.

"Miao-o-ow!"

"I'm Tom, your wish cat," he seemed to say.

"It's a mistake," cried Holly.
"I wished for a kitten."
Tom didn't think Holly
had made a mistake.

He rubbed his torn ear
against the window and
howled so loudly it
made him cough and
splutter.

"Miao-o-ow, o-o-w, o-o-w!"

Holly hid under her
duvet, hoping that
he'd go away.

The next morning, Tom
was still there, waiting for
her outside the cat flap.
He wanted to come in, and
he had brought her a present
of a smelly old piece of fish.

"Yuk!" said Holly. She picked it
up and dropped it in the dustbin.
Tom looked puzzled. "Bad cat,"
she said, shooing him away.

"Go on, go home!" said Holly,
walking across to her swing.

But Tom was
there before her.
He sharpened
his claws on
the swing . . .

and washed his
coat noisily,
pulling out bits
of fur and spitting
them everywhere.

At lunchtime, Tom sat on the
window sill, watching Holly eat.

She broke off a piece of her sandwich and passed it out to him through the cat flap. Tom wolfed it down, purring all the while.

In the afternoon, a cold wind swept through
the garden, and Holly had to wear her jacket
and scarf. Tom didn't seem to feel the cold.
He followed her around . . .

chasing leaves . . .

balancing along the
top of the fence . . .

showing off.

Soon it was time for Holly
to go indoors to tea.

"Bye then, Tom," she said,
and stroked his tatty head.

Tom followed her across to the door
and settled himself by the cat flap.

That evening, it snowed.
Gleaming pompoms of
snow danced in the air.

Outside the cat flap,
Tom curled himself
into a ragged ball to
keep warm. Soon there
was a white cushion of
snow all over the
doorstep, and on Tom.

Holly heard him miaowing miserably.
She ran to the cat flap and held it open . . .

Tom came in, shaking snow all over
the kitchen floor.

"Poor old Tom," said Holly.

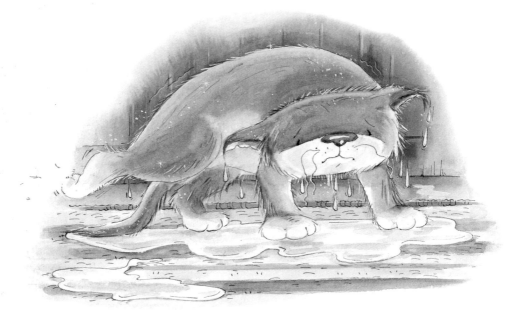

He ate a large plate of food, and drank
an even larger bowl of warm milk.
Tom purred louder than ever when
Holly dried him with the kitchen towel.

Soon Tom had settled
down, snug on Holly's
bed. Holly stroked his
scruffy fur, and together
they watched the
glittering stars.

Then, suddenly,
another star fell. Holly
couldn't think of a
single thing to wish for.
She had everything she
wanted. And so had Tom.

Have you caught up with these Two Troublesome Tales from Little Tiger Press?

Join Shaggy Dog as he itches and scratches his way through an action-packed day. And giggle at Titus the goat as he eats his way through *everything*!

For information regarding the above title or for our catalogue, please contact us:
Little Tiger Press, 1 The Coda Centre, 189 Munster Road, London SW6 6AW
Tel: 020 7385 6333 • Fax: 020 7385 7333
E-mail: info@littletiger.co.uk • www.littletigerpress.com